The **Sophia Day**® Creative Team-
Kayla Pearson, Timothy Zowada,
Stephanie Strouse, Megan Johnson, Mel Sauder

Designed by Stephanie Strouse

Published and Distributed by MVP Kids Media, LLC
Mesa, Arizona, USA
Printed by RR Donnelley Asia Printing Solutions, Ltd
Dongguan City, Guangdong Province, China
DOM June 2018, Job # 03-003-01

help me
BECOME ™

Becoming *Honest*
& Overcoming *Lying* ™

REAL

mvpkids ®

Lock Up Lying ™

SOPHIA DAY ®

Written by Kayla Pearson   Illustrated by Timothy Zowada

TABLE OF CONTENTS

Liam Learns
to be a
Doctor

Buh-Bump! Buh-Bump!

Liam was excited to hear a heart beat as he used a stethoscope.

This year Liam was finally old enough to go to La Paz City Children's Hospital with his mom, Dr. Johnson, for *Bring Your Child to Work Day.*

Everything they did was so much **better** than Liam expected!

Liam got to see and touch real organs!

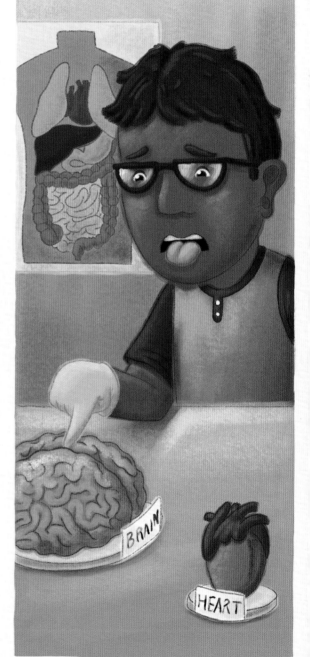

BRAIN

HEART

He learned

where to feel for a pulse on his wrist.

They even performed

a mock surgery in an operating room!

Next, the group followed their leader into the MRI room. The leader explained how **important** technology is to doctors.

"Machines like this one help doctors understand what is going on inside your body, things they can't see from the outside." They each took turns lying on the MRI table.

As Liam was waiting his turn, he noticed some buttons on the machine. One button was flashing orange. Curious about what would happen, Liam pressed the button.

Beep! Beep! Beep!

The table began to slowly slide into the machine.

The leader came over right away and pushed the button again. The table stopped. She looked at Liam and the two other kids standing closest to the button.

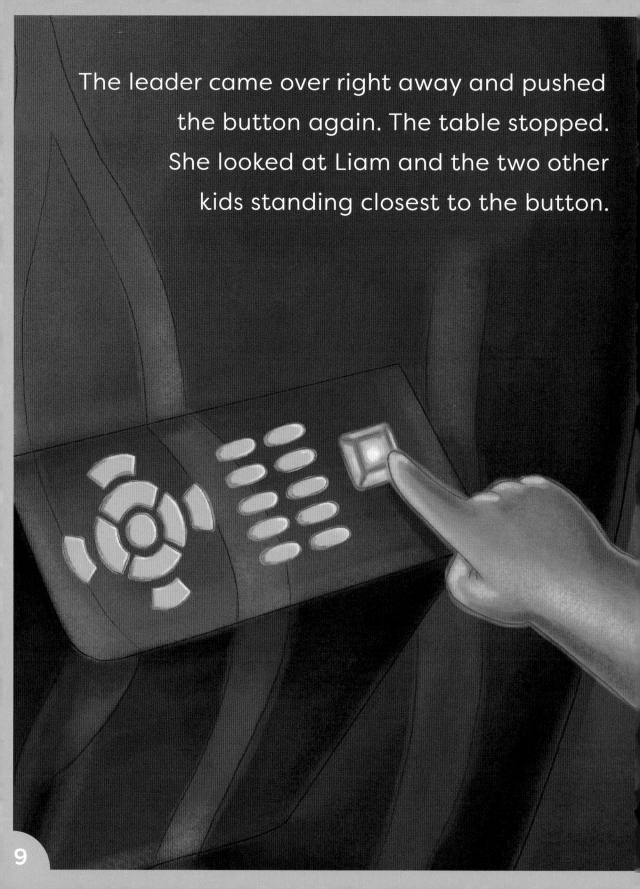

"I'm going to ask which one of you pressed the button, and I need you to **choose to tell the truth.**"

Liam *didn't* want to tell the truth.

He didn't want to get in trouble.

What if she made him **leave** the group and **go home?**

But what would happen if he **lied?**

Liam looked at the other kids. If he said he didn't do it, would they all **get in trouble?**

Liam didn't want anyone else to get in trouble for something he did. Liam decided to tell the truth. "It was me. I pressed the button."

"Thank you for **telling the truth,** Liam. Pressing buttons could get someone hurt. You'll need to stay close to me and be my helper for the rest of the day. I'll help you keep your hands safe."

Slowly, Liam walked to the front of the line with the leader. Even though he was a little embarrassed, he was glad he didn't lie and get the other kids in trouble.

The rest of the day, Liam learned a lot about doctors and how telling the truth to doctors is so important.

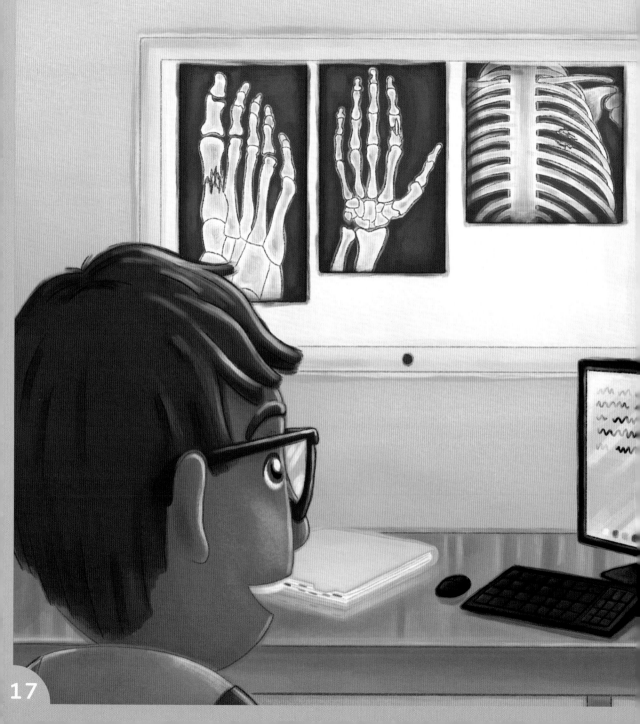

When the day was finished, he told his mom about everything he learned... and he told the whole truth about what happened. His mom was proud he chose to be honest.

THINK & TALK ABOUT IT

Liam Learns to be a Doctor

Discuss the story...

1. Why was Liam at the hospital?

2. What kinds of things did Liam learn?

3. Why did Liam press the button?

4. What might have happened if Liam lied?

5. How did Liam feel when he told the truth?

*For additional tip and reference information, visit **www.realMVPkids.com**.*

Discuss how to apply the story...

1.   What does it mean to tell the truth?

2.   Why do you think it is important to tell the truth?

3.   Tell about a time you had to choose to either tell a truth or a lie.

4.   Which did you choose? Why?

5.   Even if it means you might get in trouble, will you choose to tell the truth?

FOR PARENTS & MENTORS: *Knowing how to respond to a child who has lied depends on their developmental stage. Kids choose to lie for different reasons at different ages. Children as young as toddlers can tell lies to get something they want, but may not understand the concept of lying. By the time kids are in preschool they may begin making up stories as their way of processing new ideas. As kids enter into the elementary school years, they can understand the difference between telling the truth, a lie and story telling. At this age, they may tell more lies to see what they can get away with.*

Children often lie to avoid punishment. Asking questions when you already know the answer may corner a child into telling a lie. Instead, present the question in a way that encourages the child to choose to tell the truth. When the child chooses to tell the truth, be sure to praise their honesty.

20

Julia's BIG Shot

Julia sat on the sideline of the La Paz City High School soccer team practice. Her papá coached the team, and he would sometimes bring Julia and her little brother Victor to watch. Julia and Victor loved the chance to play soccer with the **big** kids.

Toward the end of practice, Julia and Victor would come onto the field to play with the team.

At the penalty line, Julia kicked the soccer ball hard, but **it went over the goal.**

"Nice try, Julia!

Next time lean over the ball more.
Victor gets a shot now!" said Julia's papá.

"Victor! Victor! Victor!"

the team started to chant. Victor *always* seemed to get more attention from the team.

This made Julia feel *jealous*.
"Urrgg. I wish I would have made that goal," thought Julia.

Victor shot the ball low
and to the corner.

Victor scored!

The team ran up
and gave Victor
high fives.

"Practice is over! Good job tonight team!"
Everyone ran to the sideline to grab some water.

"Way to go little man!"

"We could use your awesome skills on our team."

"Are you sure you're only five?"

28

Julia did not like that he was getting all the attention so she blurted out, "I scored three goals at my game last Saturday! And I can juggle the ball fifty times without it dropping!"

She had only scored **one** goal and she **wasn't** very good at juggling. She just wanted to impress them. She wanted them to see she was a great soccer player, too.

"Fifty times?! Wow, that's pretty impressive. Let's see you do it," one of the players challenged her. Julia tried to get out of it, but the players insisted she show them.

"One, two, three, four..."

The team counted out loud with each bounce. She tried a couple of times but never made it past ten. She kept trying, but the players slowly began to leave.

Finally, Papá came over to speak with Julia. "Julia, why did you tell the team you could do something when you are not able to do that yet?"

"You are a great soccer player. Everyone misses a shot sometimes, but that does not make you a bad player. You shouldn't lie to make yourself look better than others."

35

"I wish I would have never said that.
Now, I look even worse."

"You should have congratulated your brother and been honest about your skills. That would have impressed the team. Remember, you don't have to prove yourself to others, but practice to improve yourself for you."

"Yeah, you are right," Julia said.
Her papá gave her a hug. Then, she helped him pick up
the cones and carry the equipment back to the car.

THINK & TALK ABOUT IT

Julia's Big Shot

Discuss the story...

1. What was Julia doing at the soccer field?

2. What happened that made Julia feel jealous?

3. Why did Julia choose to lie?

4. How did lying make things worse?

5. What should Julia have done differently?

Discuss how to apply the story...

1. Do you think the other players will trust what Julia says next time?

2. Was there a time when you lied and someone found out? How did lying make things worse?

3. Julia felt embarrassed when she missed the goal. Tell about a time when you felt embarrassed.

4. Julia felt jealous when her brother was getting more attention from the team. Tell about a time when you felt jealous.

5. What is something else you can do when you feel embarrassed or jealous other than lying?

FOR PARENTS & MENTORS: *Any healthy relationship, whether between family members or friends, is based on trust. Without honesty, trust is not possible. This is one reason why teaching a child to tell the truth is so important. Talk with your child about how lying doesn't help, along with sharing the negative consequences of lying. Oftentimes, lying has natural consequences, such as the loss of trust or the embarrassment of getting caught (like what happened in the story with Julia). When this happens, be sure to talk with your child about how being honest would have been better. Admit that telling the truth may take courage, but help them recognize that it always works out better in the end.*

Frankie and Leo's Police Station Tour

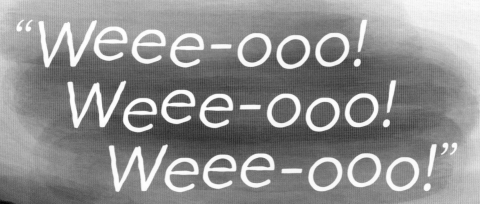

"Weee-ooo!
Weee-ooo!
Weee-ooo!"

Frankie and Leo's dad
was showing them the sirens
on his police car. Today, their dad was
giving them a tour of the new police station.

After showing them his police car,
their dad recorded their fingerprints.

He took them to an empty
cell where people who
are arrested would stay.

He even introduced them to two police dogs named BOLO and CODIS.

"Boys, wait over here. I need to talk to my partner for just a minute. I'll be right back."

"This has been the best day ever!" Frankie said to Leo.

"Let's play cops and robbers while we wait!"

Leo pretended to be a police officer chasing Frankie.

Leo lost control of his walker and banged into a filing cabinet. Everything went **crashing to the floor.**

Frankie quickly helped Leo get up and made sure he wasn't hurt.

"Boys, *what happened*?" asked their dad as he rushed over.

Frankie and Leo looked at each other. Leo decided to speak up. "Well, Dad, I..."

Frankie quickly interrupted. "We were standing here waiting for you. Then, a police dog came running through here. He knocked Leo into the cabinet."

CAPTAIN RANDALL ROY

Their dad looked at them and then glanced around the office.

He knelt down and said,
"Boys, you know as a police officer it is my duty to **protect the** truth. I am trained to know when someone is *lying.* I'm going to give you one more chance to tell me the truth."

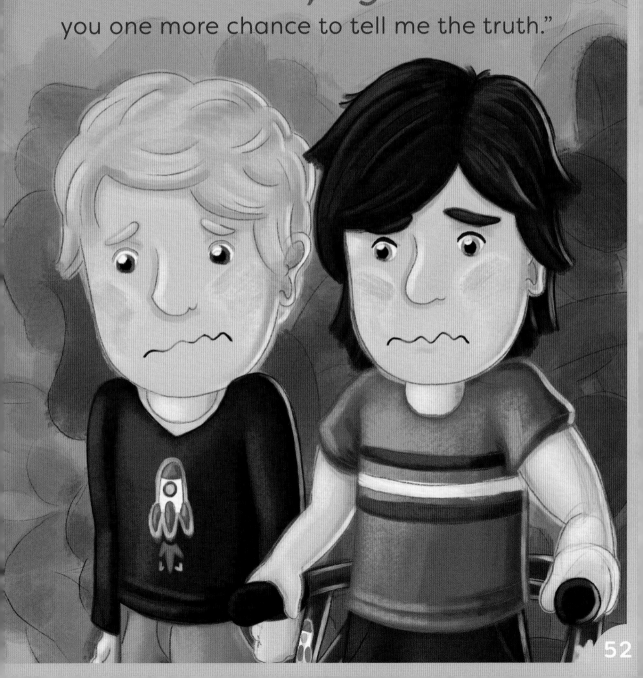

"It was my fault, but it was an accident.
Frankie only said that to protect me,"
Leo admitted.

"Thank you Leo for telling the truth.
You both know I would
rather hear the truth **over a** lie.
No matter what happens, always tell the truth."
Frankie and Leo nodded their heads.

"Do you want to see where we keep people who try to hide the truth?"
"Yeah!" Frankie and Leo answered.

Their dad led them to an empty cell. He pretended to lock them up and throw away the key.

"Now, it's time to meet Police Captain Roy."
Their dad led them to the captain's office. The police
captain presented them with their very own deputy
badges. He told them that it should remind them to
always stand up for the truth.

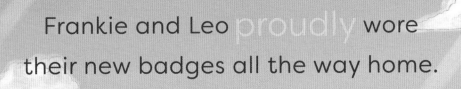

Frankie and Leo proudly wore
their new badges all the way home.

THINK & TALK ABOUT IT

Discuss the story...

1. What did Frankie's dad show them at the police station?

2. Should Frankie and Leo have been running around the police station when their dad told them to wait?

3. What happened because they were running around?

4. Why did Frankie lie?

5. What does their dad always want them to do?

*For additional tip and reference information, visit **www.realMVPkids.com**.*

Discuss how to apply the story...

1. Even though Frankie was trying to protect Leo from getting in trouble, do you think Frankie should have lied?

2. Have you ever lied to protect someone?

3. How can telling the truth, even if someone gets in trouble, still be caring?

4. Do you think your parents or guardians would rather hear the truth or a lie?

5. Part of a police officer's job is to protect people. Why do you think it is important to tell them the truth?

FOR PARENTS & MENTORS: When children have the courage to tell the truth even when they know they've done something wrong, be sure to praise their honesty. Show them the value of honesty by being a good example of what it means to be honest. Also, take the time to point out role models (personally connected or famous) who valued honesty and told the truth. One of the most commended traits of responsible leaders is honesty.

Teaching kids to respect the law and authority figures is important. Authority figures are responsible to help keep the community safe. This requires the help and cooperation of people within the community. A child's perception of authority often mirrors their parents' view, so be sure to set a good example in how you talk about them. Explain to your child that obeying and telling the truth helps keep the community safe.

Meet the

mvpkids®

featured in
Lock Up Lying™
with their families

LIAM JOHNSON

**DR. DASHA
JOHNSON**
"Mom"

ESME JOHNSON
Sister

JULIA ROJAS

**COACH
SANDRO ROJAS**
"Papá"

VICTOR ROJAS
Brother

FRANKIE RUSSO

LEO RUSSO

SERGEANT LORENZO RUSSO
"Dad"

YONG CHEN

LEO RUSSO

FRANKIE RUSSO

JULIA ROJAS

GABBY GONZALEZ

ANNIE JAMES

AANYA PATEL

BLAKE JAMES

SARAH COHEN-GOLDSTEIN